# The Suitcase

For Marylène, Rafaël and Lucille.
And for everyone who started a new life far away.

First published in 2019 by Nosy Crow Ltd
The Crow's Nest, 14 Baden Place, Crosby Row, London SE1 1YW
www.nosycrow.com

ISBN 978 1 78800 447 3 (HB)
ISBN 978 1 78800 448 0 (PB)

Nosy Crow and associated logos are trademarks and/or
registered trademarks of Nosy Crow Ltd.

A CIP catalogue record for this book is available from the British Library.

Printed in China
Papers used by Nosy Crow are made from wood grown in sustainable forests.

10 9 8 7 6 5 4 3 2 1

# The Suitcase

Chris Naylor-Ballesteros

A strange animal arrived one day
looking dusty, tired, sad and frightened.

He was pulling a big suitcase.

Hey!
Hi there!
What's in
your suitcase?

My
suitcase?

Well, there's a teacup.

A
teacup?

That's a
big suitcase
for a little
teacup!

Yes,
I suppose
it is.

But there's a table for my teacup
and a wooden chair for me to sit on too.

There's a
table
and a chair
in your
suitcase?
Impossible!

Well,
it's his
suitcase.

But a
table and
chair?
Really?

Yes.

And there's a little kitchen in a
wooden cabin where I make my tea.
That's my home.

It's on a hillside surrounded by trees
and on a clear day you can see the sea.

It's all there, in my suitcase.

But I'm sorry,
I'm really very,
very tired.
I've been
travelling for
a long time
and come
a long way.
I must have
a little rest . . .

What a
strange animal!
I've never seen
anything like
him before.

Neither have I.
But we really
should let him
sleep for a
while.

Well, I don't
trust him.
How do we
know he's
telling the truth?

There's only
one way to
find out . . .

Someone pass me a big rock. We're going to break open the suitcase and see what's inside.

Maybe we
should.
We need
to know
the truth.

You can't
do that.
It's not ours!

In no time at all,
the suitcase was open.

See?
A broken
teacup and an
old photograph.
He lied to us!

Well,
no . . .
h-he did say
there was
a teacup.

Yes.
And now his
suitcase is
broken too!

What will he
think of us?

Meanwhile the sleeping stranger
dreamed about running away
and hiding, about climbing over
mountains . . .

. . . and swimming across deep waters.

And he dreamed about his suitcase
and all that he had inside it.

When he finally woke up, he couldn't
believe what the other animals had done . . .

I'm sorry
I broke
your suitcase.
We fixed it
as best we
could.

And we've
been busy
while you
were
sleeping.

We hope
you
like it.

Thank you!
It's . . .
it's perfect!

There's just
one tiny
problem . . .

. . . we're going to need
**more teacups.**